This book belongs to

_____Nava_____

____and mommy____

Written by Ronne Randall
Illustrated by Kristina Khrin

This edition published in 2008
Parragon
Queen Street House
4 Queen Street
Bath BA1 1HE, UK

ISBN 978-1-4054-9458-8
Printed in China

# Mommy's Little Girl

# PaRragon

Bath · New York · Singapore · Hong Kong · Cologne · Delhi · Melbourne

Amy loved being Mommy's little girl.

Mommy and Amy did a
lot of things together.

They drew pictures ...

they went
on picnics ...

and they read magical
stories together.

Amy loved helping Mommy around the house.
She often helped with washing the dishes . . .
and with the laundry.

"My little girl is a really good helper!" Mommy said.

Sometimes Amy and Mommy
went shopping together.
"I'm so glad I have my little girl with me,"
said Mommy.

Every week they went swimming
in their matching swimsuits!

Splash!

Sometimes Amy even dressed up in Mommy's clothes! "You really are Mommy's little girl!" everyone said.

One day, when Amy was helping Mommy make the beds, Mommy asked her to get some pillowcases from the cupboard in the hall.

Amy found the pillowcases. She also found a big pink box. Amy wondered what could be inside it.

Amy opened the box.
Inside, she found a lot of
clothes. She took some
out to look at them.

There were
tiny T-shirts . . .

pretty dresses . . .

and dainty shoes.

"These clothes are so little!" Amy thought.
"They're just the right size for my doll!"

Amy showed some of the clothes to Mommy.
"Are these doll clothes?" asked Amy.
"You can have those clothes for your
doll," Mommy replied, "but they weren't
doll clothes to begin with. They belonged
to my little girl."

Amy was puzzled. She thought
she was Mommy's little girl!

Mommy saw
Amy's worried face.
"Come downstairs,"
she said, smiling,
"and I'll show you."

In the living room, Mommy
and Amy sat down on the sofa.
Mommy showed Amy a big book
filled with photographs.

"Let's look at
this photo album
together," Mommy said.

Mommy opened the book,
and Amy saw a picture of a baby.
"That's my little girl," said Mommy.

"That's my little girl, too," said Mommy,
showing Amy another picture, this time
of a toddler in a small pool in the garden.

Amy's eyes opened wide. "That little girl is ..."
"YOU!" Mommy finished. "And the clothes in the box
were yours when you
were a baby!"

"You mean I was once as small as my doll?"
Amy asked, surprised.
"Even smaller," said Mommy.

"You are a much bigger girl now," said Mommy,
"and you will get even bigger! But you are still my
little girl—and you always will be!"
    That made Amy very happy.
And sharing a big hug with Mommy
made her even happier.

The End